FOX AND FALCON

C. Van Heyden

A VELVET GLOVES
PUBLISHING BOOK © 2013

1st Printing April 2013
2nd Printing April 2017
August 2019 Anniversary Edition

Other books by Van Heyden:

Confessions of an Alien Marooned on Earth – Vol 1

Sellier – Book III – Confessions of an Alien…

On Conquering Things

Poetry My Mother Would've Approved

What Kids Know That Adults Have Forgot

The Reincarnation of Edgar Allan Poe

FOX AND FALCON

SEQUEL TO CONFESSIONS OF AN ALIEN MAROONED ON EARTH

A Novel by

C. Van Heyden

C. Van Heyden

Contents

Dedicated
to
"Elron"

C. Van Heyden

Recap

In CONFESSION OF AN ALIEN MAROONED ON EARTH VOL 1, Elvis Apolliani stumbles across a fellow college student on campus, which sets off a series of memories of a planet and a judgment and cruel banishment from that planet. After many sessions with Joshua, the student he encountered and now his confessor, a lay minister in training, and several séances with Madame Chartreuse, a medium, Elvis recovers clear memories of all the facts except one concerning his marooned status on Earth. In addition, the confessions permitted Elvis to regain some of his super abilities and with the use of them in giving aid to others he was able to acquire additional powers that he had on Sellier, his home planet. By the end Elvis however could not locate the means back to Sellier; neither through regressing Joshua, also a castoff from Sellier, who he thought could provide him the details of how exactly the transport took place and how to replicate the vehicle. Nor could Elvis learn through knowledge of teleportation, an alternate method of travel between planets. A subject which in its embryonic stage, he found, could admit only the tiniest of particles to be transferred and only on the surface of Earth.

C. Van Heyden

FOX AND FALCON

BOOK II

BACK IN LAYTON

C. Van Heyden

"You know who Seymour Traher was? Not likely," Elvis spoke out loud to no one in particular. 'He was the first and only man who told me, *Life is great, if you just don't weaken*.' Elvis reflected as the plane flight wearied him into daydreaming.

'He was a book salesman. He also smuggled exotic birds into the U.S., and I surmise that may have been his primary source of income. If I hadn't dodged the draft, moved to California, and under an assumed name sold encyclopedias I never would have met Seymour.' And he drifted off further.

Getting back home from China for Elvis was easy by jet plane, the contrast in civilization was not easy. He had lost his close friend and confidant to the much more civil world of Fengcheng, the small village where Joshua would eventually attain Martial Arts Master. All he had to look forward to was more searching, and to tell his findings or experiences, perhaps even his success, but no one to tell them to, he thought.

He told me (James), "No doubt my help to the local police was still something I could fall back on, but Layton, although close to the big cities was a sleepy town in the main, nothing very news-worthy happened, being a small college community. My thoughts turned now to Catherine and her father Frank, but mainly C. Could it be that I was destined to marry this filly. If I did, how could I ever then leave Earth?"

"Catherine had evolved to a much more tolerant person since our going steady party. My affinity for her increased even when I sojourned in places far from Layton. We had stayed in touch by telephone and when I returned, we consummated our desires in a week-long tryst of pure love-making that would have made a bacchanal blush."

"I discovered that Josh had given all of his notes of our sessions to you to compile. Of course, I presumed you would keep them confidential and sacrosanct."

"Frank, had somehow avoided confrontation with Stockton and was still working at MB Advanced Design Center, and as far as Catherine could tell not slated to be fired."

"I stopped by the sheriff's office just to let him know that I would be available. Sherriff Bradford told me things were quiet since that college drug related murder incident. That's how he referred to it. I felt compressed. Most of my savings was gone, the largest part used up for my excursion to China, and before that my expedition around the

U.S. to find solace and perhaps a kindred spirit who could assist my efforts to get back to Sellier."

"Catherine, when I was away did anyone call for me?"

"Not that I remember, but I was not home all day each day either."

So far I had not told Catherine about my powers, but it seemed that it was not possible to keep the secret from her. My third year at Bingham University was soon to start, my days would now be entirely filled up with class work, homework, research and perhaps a football game now and then. Oh, and church. Turning twenty was nothing, in the manner of Mark Twain, "I've done it a thousand times."

What I needed to do *a thousand times* more were acts calculated to raise the survival of one or more persons, never letting them know *how* it came about.

One night I went online to find any occult websites that I could find that might afford me information or connection to anyone like Master Chip Ty Dick. A being named *Levi* had a site that proclaimed he knew the secrets to time travel. For a small shipping fee anyone could receive his discoveries about it. I ordered the report after check ing his URL in the whois.org to see where he was probably located. Then seeing that he was overseas I optioned to download the documents.

HUNT FOR ALLIES

C. Van Heyden

Levi believes under hypnosis, by a trained operator, any person can go back in time and relive the past. He's done it many many times, he says. But I had done that already with Josh, achieved "time travel". What I needed was space travel and FAST. I emailed Levi a message about that. I got back, "Sorry, don't do space travel, AND anyway the worlds coming to an end." He added that there was a book he once read that talked about teleportation between worlds. He couldn't remember the title, but the author's name had something to do with Alice In Wonderland and Nursery Rhymes. In my research up to that moment all my research was about teleportation on Earth, which even if it did exist for bodies, it would not get me home to Sellier. I had to locate that book.

First, I checked the World-Cat online, called a dozen bookstores in New York and Los Angeles, nothing. Each time the bookseller would say, "Lewis Carroll". Lewis Carroll never wrote any books about teleportation or even mentioned it.

I hoped that being ignorant about doing one's taxes or what taxes were even about was passing. Also, stupidity about how things were made or done, and especially the mentality of those who "Just do their job to get a pay-check" were also on the decline—which mentality I believe doesn't exist outside the reactionary need to defend oneself because of one's unenviable condition. Would it be a bad thing if a majority of the population were savvy about all the important things in life, and not just the things of day to day existence? How could it not? Children in elementary schools at the turn of the 20th Century studied two languages, usually Latin and sometimes Greek and one other and could write and speak them as well as proper English. And these were children that went back to working the farm or ranch when the summer season arrived. Math was a breeze science held no mystery particularly. Children wanted to work and could work at an intelligent level until *once again* federal law was passed to *protect* them from exploitation. Shudder the thought, what that has engendered since.

Thoughts came to me rapidly: 'If I did locate it, would I be able understand it, and far more important could I build such a device except at astronomical cost?' Just like Clive Cussler in his stories has Pearlmutter, the man he goes to for arcane and obscure references—from books that are even greater in obscurity and arcaneness—I soon discovered such a person on campus. But before I could reach this person, a panic broke out amongst the senior students. It followed a report that the world in fact would be coming to end, for real this time, and the report included *scientific facts* which correlated with many ancient Mayan prophecies. This was the first time ancient and contemporary sciences congealed as one. Therefore, the illuminati of the university, the seniors of course and even some professors, were having meetings and calling for strict measures to see what could be done to save their insular world which they were sure this time was about to dematerialize.

This so disrupted class schedules and studying that the board of regents had to declare martial law.

And not too unlike my experiences on Sellier with mass hysteria and civil commotion, I was not able to contact *my Pearlmutter*.

"Catherine?"

"I'm in the shower."
"OK love just wanted to make sure you were home. I've got some strange news to tell you when you are dry."

Catherine came bounding out of her bathroom naked, wet and with wide eyes, "You got all 'A's on your examines?"

"C-A-T-H-E-R-I-N-E...the term just started."

"Well, I...what's the strange news?"

"The world is not coming to an end." Catherine still naked and dripping water, "That's great! I was planning on taking us to dinner and then to bed for some fun early tonight." Catherine had landed a job with one of the administrators at the university, and I thought for sure she had gotten wind of all the foo-fa. Apparently not.

"Yeah, well I'm all for that plan, but what I said is true no matter what you hear or from who. The edges of the sun aren't going to explode into a shower of gamma rays that will knock out all electrical and electronic devices, equipment and generators and cast us into the dark ages again and cause the poles to reverse."

"You look so cute when you get scientific with me." And back into the bathroom she went smiling and singing.

"Scientific", snapped back Elvis. 'Bloody show so far', he thought. He could not resign himself to just giving up and living the normal life. Out of 7+ billion souls, refugees from other worlds, there must be not one but several who he could contact and contact right now who knew enough to make a college try of getting back to his home planet. Getting their phone numbers or addresses and getting them in was the nut to crack.

Madame Chartreuse had aided him before in his efforts and she didn't fail him once. Could she be helpful, useful to contact more like himself was his question. Last time he asked Madame C. to locate other world beings who might have come from Sellier, she could only summon a ragtag posse of lost souls in limbo. But could she locate living beings as well, why shouldn't she? He hadn't asked her to do that, had he?

LEADS FROM MADAME C.

C. Van Heyden

Madame C. this is Elvis. Since returning from China and starting my fifth semester, I have not been able to locate anyone who remotely has a reality on my home planet, Sellier, remember? I wonder if you could do some psychic research, and I'll pay you to contact someone on Earth living that I might reach for collaboration. Just let me know their names and where they are, and I'll take it from there. Bye."

At least he was doing something, instead of taking a back seat.

Catherine did as she predicted. She took Elvis to dinner, then to bed, and they resumed their relationship as though he had never been away.

As predicted, Madame C. responded within 24 hours with a list of names and locations. Elvis got to work and plotted out the closest ones, which turned out to be only one. He had sunk his last $200 in the effort which went to Madame C. The person he isolated as reachable—and this time he wanted a vis-à-vis—lived in Texas. Elvis needed it to be a one on one, since telephones are prey to tapping and conversations are subject to clandestine recordings. If he had to, he would hitchhike his way to Texas to meet this contact. That was a skill he had developed as a teenager and got to all places North, East and South from Layton. He even hitchhiked West to his summer beach job and back and then downtown and back home when he lived in the suburbs. So

good was he at doing it in those days, that one day a beautifully tailored, chic woman picked him up in a Mercedes open convertible and took him right to the spot he was headed towards.

This guy, Marcus was his name, nicknamed Marty, lived not far from San Antonio, one of the cities Elvis had visited in his sojourns away from Layton. The sojourns before he shoved off for China and Fengcheng province, where Josh was studying with taekwondo Master Chip Ty Dick. But Elvis couldn't just up and leave during semester; he had reports and mid-term exams in a few weeks, plus he could not afford to attract undue attention during his search and until he succeeded. Thanksgiving break lasted almost two weeks. That's when he would make his way East again.

BETTING WITH FORESIGHT

C. Van Heyden

Hitchhiking was a definite fail-safe plan, but he would still need funds for living expenses and for buying information and or help. Through Catherine he might get a loan from Frank Bishop, her father. That was dicey though. Why? Because she would want to know what the dough was for, and that would blow the whole plot. Catherine might still be a mite naïve, but she was honest, and she'd have to tell her dad what the money was for. Instead, Elvis decided he would lay a small wager on the football game coming up at home. He would use one of his special powers to see the future and make a profit while testing out the ability. This was being done with purpose, and therefore OK, so it had every chance of coming off. If it did work, he would do it again but with a larger sum, after he showed his classmates that he could predict the exact final score. They would bankroll the following game bet.

Bingham had a decent football team but never had a truly winning season. Rival Cameron State probably would be victorious but not by much. The betting always included a bet on the spread of points. Elvis just looked and he saw 15 to 12 final score Cameron victorious. A bit screwy but that's what he saw. So, he bet against his own team and put $25 on a three-point loss to CS.

"Hey Dickerson!"
"What's up Elvis?"

"Got a tip on the game this Saturday..."
"Thought you weren't a better."

"Only when I'm not certain of the outcome."
"You think we'll beat Cameron?"
"No, I think...no, I know we'll lose 15 to 12. and that's what's up. And you can tell your betting friends."

"I'll tell them, but I won't bet against Bingham. In fact, I've got them as a seven point winner this weekend. You sure you don't want to change your bet?"

"Not a chance."

"Where did this tip come from, or should I ask?"

"It's kosher. I've been doing some study in the occult; you know that Nostradamus thing we touched on in Philosophy."

"Yeah, but he took drugs before he got his predictions, and many were off quite a bit, although I admit some were on the money. You're not into drugs, are you?"

"It's been all the rage on campuses since the '60's, but no I'm not into that. I do it by a method that you might call self-hypnosis."

"Well we'll see good buddy if you are Nostradamising well or not come Saturday."

Dickerson was a jock, and a pretty decent basketball forward. He lacked the ability to jump and to dunk but he sure could fire from the outside. 'The Dick' as we named him, tried to get me to join the team, but at 6-2 I would be the shortest and I couldn't shoot worth a damn. He towered over me at 6-7 without the laces on.

The day of the game Saturday morning classes were suspended, and the crowd was in the thousands, something new for Bingham. Bingham got the toss and out of the gate had a touchdown in about five minutes. It didn't bother Elvis, since the final score was already a foreseen fact. He knew it through and through. Then Cameron state scored two fairly easy touchdowns but no two-point conversions. For a second it rocked Elvis a bit since the half wasn't over; in fact, there were fourteen more minutes of regulation play left. So Bingham had seven and Cameron the twelve they would end the day with, since points can't be lost in football. Which gave Elvis a mischievous thought. Why couldn't they, and then he remembered a game like football he played on Sellier when he was growing up. It was almost the same except if a player intentionally injured another player the team lost its last score. And the team would lose its entire score if even one player gloated over a player of the opposing team receiving injury. Still another reason he wanted desperately to return to his home planet. It was much better than Earth.

When the second half began, threatening clouds, ominous clouds appeared seemingly from nowhere.

Elvis had never been at football game in the rain, and the muddy conditions that were sure to ensue made him double think the whole scheme of his to get funds for visiting Texas during Thanksgiving. Water and pigskins do not mix well, makes them slippery in the hands of quarterbacks, in the hands of the receivers trying to catch passes, in the hands of running backs causing them to fumble. It started to rain, and then it rained harder, so hard he could barely see the field and the players. Bingham needed to get only eight more points and NO MORE. Cameron needed to fumble the ball a lot and not make it near Bingham's end zone or a field goal would kill the wager, and his plans for Texas. The third quarter expired with no change in the score or the rain. It was hard to recognize the teams because their suits were getting completely muddy except the white numbers. But some of the defense players for Cameron showed the same numbers, like 88 was a line-backer and 88 was the tight end for Bingham. A short pass to the wrong 88 and....

This he could not let happen. As the clock wound down, and Bingham got more desperate to put the winning TD on the board, Elvis got a premonition that what he feared would happen was about to happen and Cameron would score instead of his team. He quickly went behind the bleachers and changed into a falcon. When the errant pass was thrown, he flew right at it and deflected it so it was not intercepted. In the rain few if any could tell what happened, it took place in an instant. Those that saw the deflection, who were close to the action said the ball wobbled. It was a bad pass. The quarterback saw it, knew something strange had happened but said nothing when he realized how close he had come to speeding the ball to the wrong 88.

Pheww. Now Bingham with less than three minutes to play had to march forty yards to a TD or the game was lost, and Elvis was lost. Yet the conversion too had to be made; but right now, they had forty to make, and in the mud, no more passing unless it was a lateral.

Dickerson showed up to gloat.

"So, you could be right Elvis, but you know Bingham hasn't scored in nearly three quarters. What makes you think they will now?"

"I could get into a long philosophic discussion with you Dick, but let's just watch and wait, OK?"

"Just to let you know, I did tell some of the frat boys and all of the betters in our circle that you were betting against Bingham."

"Glad you did, I'm looking forward to predicting the next football game as well."

"You know, if you are right the second time, you'll probably make a pile. But first you have to win today and at the score you predicted"

"I fully intend to do both."

Just then, the quarterback saw a golden opportunity and passed to the sideline flanker hat was being loosely guarded since the past eight plays were runs. He flipped him the ball and the flanker ran it in for six points. Then the conversion and the game was as good as sealed at 15 to 12.

Then,"You were right about the score, but you were wrong about who won."

"No, I am right on both counts. After we talked, I changed my bet Bingham would come from behind. The rain I didn't predict."

The Dick was speechless.

That night, Elvis took Catherine out to dinner with some of his winnings and told her all about the game and the bets. She dug football a lot, but couldn't get to the game, being staff she had to work Saturdays as well.

Now, to predict the next game and promote it loudly, repeatedly. Then a smooth exit come Thanksgiving. What story would he have to tell Catherine?

WHITE LIE

C. Van Heyden

Why was he even studying for exams, did it matter, he was headed far away from Earth. His clairvoyance, his ability to assume other shapes, his clairaudience and who knows what other powers he would regain between now and when he departed, he would take with him. But the thought lingered: what if he could not effect his departure from the information he was about to gain? He would have to make do until he could afford the capital to experiment, to discover or rediscover methods of interstellar travel. He was sure of that reality.

"Are you planning a trip Thanksgiving, love?"

"Catherine, it's for a company that I would like to work for. They're in Aerospace (which was true). They've been casting around for future technicians and my major is in space science, there's a fit."

"Isn't it a bit early to be talking employment?"

"Not when you realize that I could be finished early next year with all required subjects, graduate early, and they would fund my post graduate work on a pay-to-play basis."

"What does that mean?"

"Only, like football scouts for professional teams serve up inducements so a graduating athlete will sign with them and not another or rival team."

"That sounds pretty normal."

"It is, and when you think about it, it is simply good business if you want to hire the best for your company."

"Are they paying for your visit?"

"No, that is not something they will pay for since I'm not obligated in anyway to sign a contract with them."

"You will be gone the whole recess?"

"Just about, since I want to do a thorough job of seeing what the opportunity offers."

"I won't mention that we talked about going away Thanksgiving?"

"You are right, I'm sorry. What we can do and I would enjoy much more is if we had an even bigger getaway Christmastime, which is two and one-half weeks. How does that sound?"

"We can do that sure, I love Mt. San Jacinto. It will be warm down below and snow covered at the top should you get the hankering for a little Layton style frolicking in the white stuff."

"Not me."

"OK, we'll shop and eat at fine restaurants, within reason, and get lots of sun."

"That's me. And rent a Mercedes coupe?"

"Can your father lend you a couple of Franklins?"

"I'll squeeze him for it and tell him it's his Christmas present."

"That a girl!"

Another pheww!

It was true he had been interested in looking at the future after college, he had known of science-based firms in San Antonio, Houston, Dallas etc. So, he was safe there, completely, or was he?

C. Van Heyden

NEW ABILITIES &
CLOSE CALL

C. Van Heyden

Elvis noticed another benefit, completely unexpected, from his confessions to Joshua: he could study very much more easily now, in fact he was a fast but careful student whereas before it was a true labor. This gave him extra time to search out the other names and locations Madame C. had supplied him, on the off chance that his Texas contact proved as useless as Levi did.

One was in New York, one in France in a town named something like marmalade in sound, one in South Africa and one in Peru. Seemed distribution was rather sparse for an Earth population of seven billion plus, or that's all that Madame C. had time to attend to.

R. C. Lexington in NY sounded mysterious, whereas his Texas contact's name was Marty. France was Mssr. Velatrobe, and South Africa was definitely not a South African but an Africaner named, Gingham. In Peru he would look up a woman known as Serena Amparo.

Elvis' excitement grew as he contemplated success. He was already hip to the UFO cover ups, the suppressed inventions of brilliant men by Neathandral thinking, reactionary monopolizers of oil interests. Inventions though that were harder and harder to destroy or swallow up because of the omnipresent Internet and all that its freedoms allowed with accent on new and unusual creations, and always better methods of doing something vital.

He considered the impact of his thought: 'The proverbial genie has escaped out of the lamp, and no one, NO ONE or group could effectively stop the genie.'

Elvis contacted myself, the student Joshua had entrusted all of their session records to. I was the student who had divulged the private sessions to some of his student friends by way of Joshua's indiscretions. I had recanted later and decided to make up the damage he created by swearing to Joshua an oath to never gossip or pass on hearsay about another human being, no matter the justification. Since it was also a fraternity brother oath it was a reliable oath.

Elvis asked me to turn over the notes and records, which I did reluctantly. But Elvis saw that I was dejected. It was a big loss to, since I had achieved little in this life, and was rarely trusted. This oath meant that I was doing something vital and important and Joshua had trusted me without question once I gave his word to him. Elvis perceiving the pain of losing this trust, allowed me to be his new confessor providing that I take down Elvis' further confessions and adventures faithfully, combine all notes and session records into a manuscript. The data and experience Elvis was after was too critical to Man not to make a permanent record of the vital parts. First, Elvis pored through those notes for any clue or piece of evidence that he may have forgotten since the sessions, in hopes he might have already even a better source for hooking

up with another space traveler like himself. Nothing. He looked to promoting his next prediction for Bingham's football team.

Elvis true enough put his attention on the next game with Tempe Valley U. an out of conference team Bingham had never faced. He got that it would be a tie, 18 to 18. That didn't sound right but neither did 15 to 12. Nobody has so far as he remembered wagered a tie. But it was possible. He went with it full force. Informed Dickerson and spread the word in his classes to a few other jocks he knew bet on the games.

Then he asked Dickerson and one of his buddies for $200 that would become $1400 at 7 to 1 odds. Netting him approximately 1200.00 since he'd kick in an extra $50 for the loan. The Dick said no, he was thinking more like TVU winning because he had scouted them, and he wouldn't bet against his own team. His buddy did go for the $200 after how it went down between Cameron State and Bingham.

That was all Elvis needed really. Now it had to be 18 to 18 or one, he would lose the bet, and two he would lose credibility and three he would owe $200 which he didn't have or would likely get anytime soon.

Saturday came and this time it was already raining with gusting winds. No matter, the conditions never decided the game or the score, once Elvis locked onto the future reading. Practically no one was at the game but then again that might not be a bad

condition since it is widely known that a team's fans when they start rooting for their team to win and the other team or defense to mess up it can affect the score, sometimes in a major upset.

The first quarter, no score. Second quarter TVU almost made a TD on a trick play but the RB slipped on the turn up field and couldn't get his feet under again. Half time came and went in a heartbeat since no band could play in the rain. 2nd half, score, zero zero. Again, Elvis for an instant got that doubtful flicker in his mind. 'With the rain present and not abating, no score through the first half, how were these two teams going to put up three TDs a piece in the same amount of time?'

He presumed all scores would be TDs and no extra points. Then he decided that if could predict the score, he could look into the future and predict the way the scores would occur. Simple. He got TVU scoring and kicking an extra He got TVU scoring and kicking an extra point, then Bingham scoring and going ahead with a two-point conversion, then a field goal.

Dickerson said TVU is a better team, so the next score would be a touchdown by TVU with a two-point conversion and they would lead 15 to 11. Bingham would counter with a TD and a successful extra point, and then near the last two minutes or less TVU would be forced to kick a field goal on fourth down and tie the game.

That would leave scarcely a minute to play, but Bingham would pull a reverse in the mud that TVU tried and failed so they wouldn't be expecting it and Bingham would come out the winner with a field-goal. But Bingham couldn't make enough headway to get near to TVU goal line to kick a field goal and so the game ended as predicted: 18 to 18.

After paying back Dickerson's bud, he took Catherine out for dinner at the swankest restaurant in Layton. He could gloat, now that he had eleven hundred and fifty bucks and a reputation. Now, jocks and big betters were coming to him. The only problem is he didn't vitally need any more dough so he wasn't betting and if he wasn't betting and he didn't really need the money, it wouldn't work to forecast the next game; and that would lose a bunch of his friends and his friends' friends a ton of money. The best answer was to tell Dickerson and his friends that it was too dangerous putting himself into an hypnotic trance to predict scores, and that for his own health he would not continue to do it. This angered many of the betters who wanted a sure thing, especially the ones who hung back waiting to see if lightning struck twice. In the end it blew over as a hoax and most of the betters called it pure beginner's luck.

C. Van Heyden

MARTY

C. Van Heyden

Elvis also scored well academically, with A's on both his aeronautical physics and thermodynamics papers, plus a 94% on his calc examine. He had given up on locating that book on teleportation, at least for the time being, but he had an intuition that his understanding of these subjects he was studying and some input from the right sources he would figure it all out himself as to how to make his way back to Sellier. And as hoped Catherine wangled a promise of $200 from her father giving Elvis breathing room should he vacate all his earnings in Texas and come back with only change in his pockets.

He would go by Greyhound, keeping more of his funds so that if he needed to buy privileged or confidential information, he could do so with fewer worries. Elvis even packed several meals into a picnic cooler to save on restaurant food and tips.

The man he would meet, Marty, said he'd meet him at the bus station in San Antonio and take him to a hotel, Best Western class. When he arrived, he met a squat somewhat rotund man about fifty with thinning hair, but a large smile and comforting eyes.

"How went the bus trip?"

"You're Marty?"

"Yep, always have been."

"It went fine, I've been out this way before."

"So, you know San Antone, do you?"

"Pretty good, I spent a week here last year and got to see a lot of real estate, you might call it."

"Well, then I won't bother to show you around, we can just meet tomorrow morning for breakfast, and you can get some rest from what I believe was a twenty-hour bus ride, correct?"

"Closer to twenty-two, do you ride Greyhound?"

"No, I just looked at the schedule for your arrival, and it told me duration of travel time."

"It was a long one, but the seats are comfortable and of course anyone can sleep if they want. For myself, I just napped now and then. But I would like to get a fresh start in the morning and get into my hotel room for a shower."

"Sounds very good, I'll see you in the morning. BW has a great breakfast in a not so bad restaurant downstairs."

"See you then Marty."

"See you tomorrow Elvis."

Elvis liked hotels, motels. He loved not having to clean up messes or worry about fresh towels and fresh sheets, they were just there. And cable T.V. was always included. He tried to catch the results of the last game of the season for Bingham, but it was too late, the sports station had stopped reporting scores earlier. So, he showered a hot shower and hopped into bed. It wasn't long before the sawing of logs could be heard softly.

Next morning was a beautiful one with fleecy clouds and a few gusts of wind to make the fall leaves scurry into small piles. Dressing warmly, Elvis went downstairs for breakfast to meet Marty, it was 8:00AM.

Marty signaled him over to a table in the rear of the restaurant.

"How was your rest?"

"Quite good, I always fall asleep faster on fresh clean sheets. It reminded me of a feather bed I slept in, in Syracuse one night at this adorable bed and breakfast. After having a scrumptious meal complete with fresh vegetables out of the garden, I was conveyed to this bedroom that sported a large four poster with down pillows and comforter, even the mattress was down, I think. I fell asleep in a minute."

"I'm glad you're rested. I'm glad because what I'm about to reveal to you will probably stand your hair on end like during a thunderstorm's lightning."

"I think I can take it."

"Here goes then..."

"Wait, is this going to be verifiable data?"

"Seeing is believing, right?"

"That's what I'm looking for."

"As I was saying, I travel a bit. In my travels I made it to the Bosphorus area, do you know where that is?"

"Vaguely...in Europe?"

"Not precisely. It's near the Dardanelles and connects the Black Sea with the Mediterranean, and its fame is that it is a place of legend. One of the legends is it was impassable because of giant rocks that were awash in its waters. What I discovered, since it had been a hobby of mine to climb mountains, is that there is some kind of transfer point for beings outside this galaxy there."

"By what you're saying, this find is not known about at all?"

"Only those who are looking for it will find it, that's what I am saying."

"Continue."

"Well it is well hidden in a mountain pass, and I searched. Yeah did I search a long time to find it. You see I believe, let's say I have had a suspicion about extra-terrestrials for as long as I can remember. Something happened when I was young that made me remember a past existence, and it scared me somewhat but not enough to shut off the memory. I was six."

"Marty, when we talked briefly by phone, I told you why I wanted to see you, but I didn't tell you how I came to have your name and number. You never asked either."

"That's because I can see a person telepathically and know whether they are telling me the truth or not. And I've had that ability since I was six or younger."

"So, you knew at once that I was not from Earth?"

"I didn't say that, only that your request was legit, and not some plot to discredit me or trap me."

"I got your name from a medium, a medium who has checked out completely for real, completely capable in her art."

"I don't doubt it for a moment. There are persons in this world who have such abilities we never suspect, and I for one having telepathic skills I would be the first to embrace the notion that a good number of individuals must have similar qualities."

Tell me more about this place you discovered."

"The approach and entrance are high up enough to discourage most climbers, and if you have ever seen the sheer walls that mountain goats climb up and down with no fear, then you know the kind of terrain I'm talking about."

"Yes, I get what you're telling me, rough country."

"Precisely. So that if you have the heart—the determination to arrive—you'll get there in one piece. Once there you'll think there's "nothing here"; you'll think that, but you'll be very wrong. I brought a metal detector and a Geiger counter. And with those instruments I got readings way off the dial for both. That's the other danger. Radioactive material."

"How did you survive it?"

"I almost didn't. I did get sick. But fortunately like a G-O-O-D boy scout I came prepared. Since I was carrying a Geiger-counter, naturally I brought a lotion containing aloe vera and calendula which is effective against radiation burns. Only good for low doses. Which is why I got sick. Unless you can operate in a water sealed uniform, like a diver's wet suit you will probably get sick too. But you'll recover after a few weeks, if you don't stay too long."

"Sounds very adventurous."

"Oh it is very adventurous. I aged about five years.'"What do you want in exchange for the exact location and maps?"

"Nothing, now that we've met. So, you say you're not from here—where then?"

"A planet called Sellier and it's in the direction of the Constellation Bootes and very distant."

"Well, I make no promises, but I'll provide you with exact directions for when you land in Turkey."

"What did you see when you got inside the mountain?"

"I'm going to let you find that out for yourself, you wouldn't believe me if I tried to tell you. Remember, don't stay around there long"

"Not a hint, so I won't be charred by the experience if it's too much?"

"I can tell you that you will see contraptions that couldn't possibly be made by earth men, and you'll hear things that you have never heard before, so also take ear plugs. I didn't think of that, and it's another reason I got sick."

"OK, so that's it I go and find the place you've been describing to me. What of contacting the beings?"

"I don't know about that. I wasn't looking to get off this planet anytime soon, as I presume you are."

"OK, did you see any of them?"

"Yes, I did, and they are not too different than you or I.   But they don't communicate with their mouths, get it?   So, if you're not telepathic you wouldn't be able to reach them."

"That poses a serious problem to me. But it's my problem."

"Let me have the data and I'll keep it secret. You know I will."

"Meet me tomorrow here, same time."

BANK ROBBERY

C. Van Heyden

Elvis was elated and dejected at the same moment. He had been successful hearing the thoughts of Stockton, the bum manager over Frank, Catherine's father at the MB Advanced Design Center; but these beings are from other worlds. He doubted, and he didn't know why, that he could receive their thoughts, much less communicate to them. What did make for some joy was that such a place existed apparently, and he could get to it with some effort. Marty didn't have the true data he was looking for, only where to go to get it or to get back to Sellier. Still a long shot and far away.

When Marty handed over the maps and directions, he also gave Elvis the name of the radiation lotion and where to buy some. Elvis wanted to pay him for his time, but Marty wouldn't go for it. Marty would be happy if he succeeded, or if Elvis didn't at least destroy the maps and directions and let him know that he did.

By simple math, Elvis calculated that he would need about four times the bankroll he had to launch an expedition overseas. That meant working all summer and if lucky have enough to start in the fall next year.

'God', he thought. 'I just don't know if I can wait that long.'

In the next days, Elvis made his way back to Layton. But before he did, a bank robbery had occurred only blocks from his hotel, done in the manner of the old west too. Seems two men with kerchiefs over their faces up to their eyes came into the San Antonio Federal Bank building with six-guns blazing, shot a few tellers in the shoulders to make sure no one went for the buzzers under the counter, and made off with $200,000.00 in bills and traveler's cheques. The police had no leads and no clues.

Elvis stepped in and offered his services, telling the chief detective on the case to call Sheriff Bradford in Layton for corroboration of his skills. Having done so, Elvis was sworn in as a temporary deputy of the Bexar County Sheriff. He went right to work at the bank putting his attention on the time the alleged bank robbers had entered the premises and shot up the joint. In a few minutes, he was able to perceive that the assistant manager was in on the heist. Normally, the vault would not be open, but this time the assistant manager had contrived to have it so when the gun men barged in and demanded the money.

He relayed this info to the detectives on the case and they brought in the assistant manager who folded after only an hour of interrogation.

This time, Elvis was rewarded and cited in the newspapers for his commendable action.

'Chalk up one more good deed for posterity, even though it was a type of negative gain,' mused Elvis. It seemed to him at that moment that positive gain should be his major thrust in life, not merely counterbalancing or correcting bad things.

What were the positive things in life? Inventions, discoveries, art, manufacturing, harvesting—and of course planting first—education leading to proficiency and productivity. There were lots more.

Elvis added the $500 CD reward the bank gave him to his total funds and headed back to Layton a winner. Home, he relayed all the details of his trip, substituting Marty's name with various contrived names of heads of personnel departments and told Catherine mainly about the reward for helping apprehend the evildoers in San Antonio.

"So, did you land a position?"

"Not exactly, but I got a good lead. It seems there was a bit of hype I didn't quite pick up on originally at college when I heard about the pay-to-play offer."

"How so?"

"Seems I didn't get all the info I needed, and it turns out there's a big investment on my part starting with a change of location at my expense before anything more happens."

"You mean they want you to move at your expense to Texas before they sign you on?"

"Pretty close. That's the job market these days. They had too many promising candidates wash out in the first six months, breaking their contracts. They want to see tangible production first."

"OK, so you're not in a hurry to finish college then?"

"That's the size of it my sweet."

"Can we talk about Christmas now?"

"Sure, I was hoping we would."

FORTUNE TELLING

C. Van Heyden

Christmas came and Christmas left, but the hunger Elvis felt didn't. Even the thought of robbing a bank came to him in a sheer moment of desperation, but he laughed it off as absurd. 'In the old days' he was reminded 'a guy could get aboard a tramp steamer to practically anywhere, as long as he was willing to experience stinking quarters, sea sickness, bad food, hard deck labor or freezing night watches.'

He had had such an experience, which when reviewing brought up a confession, and perhaps it is where the errant thought of robbing a bank came from. So, he wrote it down and mailed it to me (James): "Put in the record that in and around 1930-ish I was made assistant purser on a steamer out of Boston Harbor bound for South Africa. They gave me a job of doling out the pay in envelopes for the crew, and I managed to embezzle several hundred dollars. By the time they found out, I had jumped ship in Durban and signed up with another outbound vessel heading back to New York."

The new year brought Elvis to face another semester with no hope of getting enough free time to procure a job where he could earn the wherewithal to get over to Eurasia and locate the teleportation station. Catherine was hinting at engagement again, after a very intimate and prolonged Christmas celebration with Elvis as her only consort. Too bad Elvis was above it, he could easily have photos taken of Catherine semi-naked and in the buff and get a spread in Playboy, then take his cut as her manager. Exploiting women was still a sous réserve de lombre.

Then quite accidentally Elvis became aware of something he was already doing that others would enjoy and that he could charge for: fortune telling. Only it wouldn't be long range fortune telling. More like what the wagering on football games consisted of, all short-term and all to make others some extra cash or better prevent them from losing it. So, they wouldn't mind parting with some cash up front, and he would be guaranteed a good deal of repeat and new customers without advertising, once he got it started. He'd put an ad in...not the local paper but one in the big city in a cheap local paper and see if he got any bites, similar to how Madame C. promoted. He could do all by telephone and use an Internet email for transfer of funds.

He placed an ad in the San Francisco Bee stating, "Want to make sure you never place a losing bet at the casinos or on football? Call for free demonstration. Anonymity guaranteed." And he started receiving requests almost immediately. He was doing it so he could get the necessary funds collected to pay for his expedition, so it was ethical, meaning it benefited more than it disadvantaged.

Within a month he had the four grand he needed for plane fare, mountain climbing gear which he'd purchase when he arrived, for food and hotel accommodations and spare in case of injury or_____? Now, to clone himself and make his way to the threshold to the orient, the land of the Arabian nights and magic, Turkey. Elvis realized it was still a shot in the dark and that more than likely he would have to return, so he bought a round-trip ticket for May, the soonest year-end exams would be over, and he could exit. This time he would blatantly tell Catherine the truth, but only enough to make for a clean departure.

C. Van Heyden

COUNSELOR TO
THE LOST

C. Van Heyden

Now Elvis hadn't done much in his efforts to improve the lots of others, since returning from the orient, just that one incident in San Antonio, which again was negative gain. He told me that if he had a great deal of money, he would open a foundation as many wealthy and famous persons do, Yet, even so that kind of contribution wouldn't net him any tangible increase in powers, and that was his last thought on the matter. He had nearly five months left in which to exercise his talents, where doing so would somehow lift another's life from stagnation or even, if it mattered, a normal good level to an even much higher level. That would be a positive gain—much like individuals who take up chess and sharpen their mental skills and even their ability to play a game.

Predicting when not to place bets fell obliquely into the above category, when it was done for the average Joe, but wasn't strong enough to cause any release of his other latent abilities. Doing it for the compulsive gambler, who Elvis carefully tried to screen and eliminate was no gain at all. He considered that a loss. Now, it occurred to Elvis that one of the major downfalls of individuals, as he saw it, was indecision. Even above average intellects were deficient in the courage to take action based upon a firm decision, with the decision ascendant in all cases. We can cite Joshua's decision to relocate to an unknown province and unknown environment in China after he made the decision to reverse his life goals, a major decision in truest sense. This was an excellent area, a fertile area for Elvis to explore.

There were many students that he knew that were just going through the motions without any solid goal in mind as to what they were going to do with their education, or for that matter with their lives. There were school career counselors, sure, but these cats were often just senior

students in their last year at the university, and some if not many were in the same boat, trying to help themselves find direction as much as to help the freshman and sophomores. I know, I was one. The standard tests for aptitude told only where a student has abilities not which life goals he or she should strive the hardest to achieve. It takes...it takes whatever Joshua got a hold of to settle completely which path to take and to pull out all the stops, no matter what.

Since Elvis could pick up the thoughts of a person when in their presence. He began counseling one student at a time, one student he selected that he liked, and thought would be fairly easy to counsel. No druggies, no criminal types, at least not at first. For free. He started with me, since I knew Joshua.

I was not an easy first. He tried to get me to recall a previous existence and all I got was blackness. Then he asked me if there was anything in the blackness that wasn't entirely black. After a while something showed, very hazy and I couldn't describe it. So, then he asked if I could recall a past death. Now, that was something I could get something on and from there we were off and running as the saying goes. Since this is not my confessions, I'll just tell you what came of it that was very satisfying and liberating for myself. I had always had a belief that everyone was a phony, meaning no one was ever really sincere, it was all a show, a put on, feelings, expressions, manners, the whole bit. That ended. Naturally I had told my parents that I was going to college to become an architect like my father was so they would pay for everything; when, in fact I have always wanted to be a filmmaker / producer, making the blockbusters and living the high life. I was being the phony that everyone else I thought was.

Next up was Ted Larkin. Seems Joshua had put him and a few of his friends through the grinder about past life existences. Ted even got sick during his sessions, though he wouldn't tell Josh about it. Elvis got him, and he too was a toughy, but finally he came up with a string of previous lives and if he were here, I'd ask him if it was alright to divulge what he saw and learned in that one session. He similar to Joshua up and left Layton.

Left for New York City, and told me he was going on Broadway and act for the rest of his life on the stage. Frankly that scared me because he looked nothing like an actor nor did he, when I knew him, have the personality of an actor. Ted, if anything had been a jerk-off and very cynical. Then, sometime around Valentines' Day, Elvis quit, he was burnt out he told me. He had salvaged probably a dozen students at Bingham. So that part of his life came to an end.

Instead of continuing in hopes of his quest for full return of his native powers, Elvis decided to begin his egress. First, he dropped hints with Catherine about the coming overseas expedition, not mentioning its true purpose but only that he was interested in traveling throughout Europe and Western Asia to fulfill a lifelong dream he had. Catherine of course could not be included since she had work beyond the college semester plus the way Elvis told it he would be moving so fast to cover so much ground that it would be uncomfortable to invite another along. He could only operate by himself at that speed. Since C. knew he had taken off the previous summer on a tour of the states this was believable, but it wasn't all right with her.

From Feb 14th to May 7th, final exams nothing else of note transpired for Elvis or Catherine. The day came when he kissed her goodbye at the airport and told her he would try to send a letter or call at least once each week. When he landed in Istanbul airport Elvis made his way to a tiny hotel Marty had included in his notes, a hotel that was the same when he had landed there. Elvis was packing about a hundred pounds of climbing equipment and special high protein food that climbers use to stay strong on long treks. If it had been in the winter, he would have had to also take with him a Coleman stove for sure heating at night to keep from freezing. Still, the nights in the high mountains, Marty told him, would not be comfy, so bring winter weight gear. The maps supplied by Marty were clear, showing relative altitudes of mountains and where there were dense forests to avoid. Getting to the base of the mountain would require hiring a car and driver since no public transportation, train, boat or plane landed anywhere near them. The one thought that plagued Elvis was falling and injuring himself and no one was there to help him. He might drag himself to safety, but he wouldn't acquire the hidden entrance that he came seven thousand miles to investigate.

Arriving in sight of his goal, he decided to rest and get plenty of it at the Gurang Hotel where his English was just barely understood by the inn keeper. The next morning, he stopped by the local police office to let the chief there know that he was a mountain climber and that he would be scaling one of two mountains on either side of the Bhanghi Pass. This way he would have a chance if he didn't come back in one piece since a search party would cover both, and at the same time would not give away the location of the teleportation station.

There was one section of the climb where Elvis had to use pitons, especially designed spikes, that when forced into the rock face made a hand hold and a step in shear walls. Only once before had he any experience with this climbing device and again it was the warmer weather that madehim confident that he could use them well to get past that barrier.

The town at 3,000 feet altitude left only 7,000 feet to climb to where the map detailed the hidden

entrance. But the last 1,000 feet was shear rock. This formidable deterrent and its remote location had kept the teleportation site's existence utterly unknown. Marty had marked the map with unique symbols to show where he had successfully navigated the treacherous climb many years ago. Elvis got through the underbrush and across small streams without incident, but when he saw the beginning of the rock face 9,000 feet up from sea level he had to draw some deep breaths. 'It could all end here' was his impression then. But even the 6,000 ft climb to that façade was more than he had previously climbed. It took five hours to finally reach it. Scratched and his hands sore in spite of special climbing gloves he looked upward and spied the peak that he had to acquire to get to the entrance. It was 2 o'clock in the afternoon. If he was successful by 5PM he would be there, with enough time to do a preliminary recon and come down to a manageable camping spot before night fall.

Elvis checked his gear, pitons, hammer, harness, carabiners, climbers-rope that he would tie off in steps as he ascended—in case he should fall—it would slow and break his rapid descent. And he made doubly sure he was carrying the aloe cream for radiation burns. It began well for the first fifty feet. Then an eighteen-inch shelf appeared overhead to complicate his upward progress. Managing that without a hitch he ascended another 300' and rested. It was 3:30PM and four hours until sunset, another hour to the summit. He was running

behind. As he told it, he got giddy as he reached the 900-foot mark of the thousand he needed to scale. His strength wasflagging. His morale was sky-high, but his expectations were tremulous, remembering what Marty told him, "You'll see contraptions that couldn't possibly be made by earth men." He not only wanted to see these machines, he wanted to cast himself off Earth in one of them.

At the highest point of the shear rock there was a fissure, large enough for a typical human to pass through. Large enough if the man or woman wasn't claustrophobic and if not wearing protective clothing didn't mind getting scratched up a lot. Elvis came out on the other side to a long corridor within the mountain top and he followed it to the room that was mentioned in the text on his map. As he approached, he removed his climbing gloves but plugged his ears with stops, just as Marty directed.

Elvis was several hundred feet inside the mountain where no one would find him if this was the end of him. Faintly, then louder as he walked further came screeching sounds and banging sounds. By the time he was at the threshold of the space that contained the teleportation system, he knew Marty was right. Once at Hoover Dam, on a field trip, he had experienced the sound of the dynamos at the fifth level down, and they were frightfully loud even when wearing ear protection given out by the tour guides. As he told it, "I must have walked through an air vent to the teleportation area, because I was looking down at an enormous contraption made of steel. A contraption which resembled nothing I had seen in my life nor in my sessions with Joshua. It seemed to be afloat in a lake of mercury. I gathered that the mercury was cooling the mammoth machine. As for the operators...I can only say that they were human sized with appendages like us but not with human faces and feet and hands, and definitely not with ears. Remembering Marty's comment about telepathic communication I sought to get as close to the main body of workers while sending out a gentle thought that I am also not from Earth and needing help getting back to my home planet."

BOSPHORUS

C. Van Heyden

Nothing. Perhaps these were workers only, the overseers remote or hidden watching and commanding. Marty said he could pick up their communication, but he didn't say whether they intercepted his. Elvis tried again, sending the simple thought, 'I am not from Earth and I'm needing help getting back to my home planet.'

That triggered something. He hadn't mentioned the name of the planet previously. Since this was a departure point, as well as ingress point for other planets where beings lived, it made some sense that the true names of planets, that would not change over time, and if known, would be permanently entered into the coordinates of the giant transporting devices. Remember, Elvis with his climbing gear on and sun goggles above his eyebrows looked a bit strange himself, his ropes and harness left at the entrance to the fissure.

Elvis began to experience an unpleasant sensation all over his body. Suddenly it came back to him that he was supposed to not linger on this spot. He took off his climbing gloves and noticed a reddening of his skin. Radiation. He realized that radiation sickness doesn't befall one immediately, and the evidence that he would be sick was in clear sight. He moved quickly to outermost perimeter of the teleportation site and headed back through the corridor vent tunnel. Emerging from the tunnel he found fresh mountain air that stimulated his senses even more. Now he could feel the pain of his burning hands and face which went unfelt inside the cavern because he was distracted first by the noise, the sights and then by the colossal apparatus and workers around it, moving as if controlled.

It was 6:25 when Elvis checked his chronometer attached to his belt. He thought that he could not repel down nor reverse his ascent before it got dark in less than an hour and a half. If he stayed at the fissure, he had a small area where he could lie down, but he didn't know and didn't think that he could stay warm enough throughout the night. Winds were blowing better than 20 mph through the crevasse he had just emerged from to escape being burned to death radioactively. If he stayed, he ran the risk of needing to be rescued if his strength was not up to retracing his steps back to the place that he started climbing the rock face. The only comforting thought left was that he had scaled to the top of the mountain, found the alleged teleporting station and if lucky will live to try again.

He decided he would repel down in stages tying off a double length of rope at each stage and looping it through his harness, a tricky maneuver for well-trained climbers. Then pull the rope as a single chord through the pulley above and attach to another pulley and continue down 'til he reached level ground. Before the start of his descent he pulled a bottle of the special lotion from his back-pack and soothed as much as he could his face and hands. Lastly, he trekked lower to a spot he noted on the way up that was tree sheltered away from the wind, where he could bed for the night. With this accomplished he rested.

In the early morning, stiff and hungry, Elvis rose and plied his way back to the Gurang Hotel and showered and rested again. Upon rising Elvis went in search of a library and municipal records vault. It seemed to him that it must be impossible for such a station to be operating close, albeit hidden, to human civilization that there had not been some contact, no matter how clandestine, at some time during the past thirty to who knows how many years.

If there had been, and in all likelihood should have been, there must be a go-between, an earth contact person or persons. 'Surely if something happened where a worker or other alien up there got badly hurt, they would need a full-fledged hospital and staff to take care of them, or did they die as just another drone bee would, immediately replaced by another dispatched through the great machine?' It was this sole thought of a go-between (planted or otherwise) which lead him further: Elvis, no matter what, wasn't returning home empty handed.

Elvis had not gotten sick as Marty had. Checking his entire peripheral nervous system (skin) he found only moderate redness under his clothes. With the salve he was back to battery and ready to extend his stay in Turkey. Elvis had an unusually strong constitution, another side benefit derived from his confessions.

Elvis looked only for old folks, villagers that had been around a long long time. Individuals that with a little cajoling and a few innocent bribes would cough up the evidence he knew had to exist.

'Bharabhas' (BHAR-A-BAS) was his name. He had lived in the village all his 89 years. Through wind and sunburned lips, he whispered of a being he met a half century ago; a being he felt was a stranger to this planet. Referring to that entity as Throgg, since he had never learned of his identity, Bharabhas told Elvis of that day. And Elvis relating to me (James) we come to revelation of how the being and the station came to be hidden all these years: a field of force. Like a jelly-fishes transparent flesh, surrounding the mountain cancelling out any invasive transmissions in either direction, perceptible to no one.

Trogg appeared that day and only one other time in recollection. He gave Bharabhas a token to remember their conversation, and he showed it to Elvis. But he would not let Elvis hold it or even examine it. Elvis drew a picture of the token and this is what he drew:

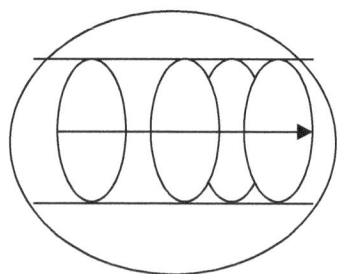

Elvis told me that when he had drawn this figure he was reminded of a play—no, a musical his father told him he'd seen when he was young and liked a long time ago named *Stop The World I Want To Get Off*, that had never been revived really, like so many other musicals from on Broadway in New York. And a song reverberated in his head at the same time:

Why don't we sing this song altogether
Open our minds let the pictures come.
And if we close our eyes together,
Then we will see where we all come from.

"It left me wondering," he emphasized, "If that was a universal symbol for teleportation." It left Elvis with an unsatisfied hunger. Elvis continued searching quietly the village for another Throgg but found no one. This was the lowest he'd been since leaving Josh and Master Chip Ty Dick in China. He dared not go back to the station without a suit of protection against the radiation. He hadn't called Catherine in five days, and it was unlikely she would be able to cheer him, what with the hot weather coming and them apart again like last summer.

He tried calling Marty, no answer, and gave up. There wasn't anything Marty could do—that's why he had given Elvis the maps with details. Marty had had his adventure and was on to other matters. Then it dawned on him. Change shape and go there as a falcon. Go there and stay there in very short periods so as not to burn up. Get as much familiarity with the operation, look for overseers, look for actual beings arriving or departing that he hadn't seen yet. And minimally discover how it was that the drones could work in that environment at all. Then, acquire a suit back home capable of withstanding that roentgen level. He wouldn't go home empty handed after all.

TELEPORTATION
STATION

C. Van Heyden

Navigating the passage, he'd come back through was tougher as a falcon, winds had increased. Elvis gets to the enormous room where the teleporters are and no one is there. Funny thing is, being a bird, the first thing Elvis does is look for other birds that might have flown in as he did, and to see if they were dead.

It occurred to him then that the room saw action only when a transfer was in progress. He must have come in last time right near when a transfer was ending, and the workers were shutting down. But now he could get around to many more locations within the cavern and much faster. Where was the central control? Where did they eat, sleep, exercise?

It didn't matter, he hadn't been able to reach them telepathically. Likely the drones were sequestered, living in shielded rooms that he could not invade. And that's how the drones, anyone, kept from getting radiation sickness or worse dying. They worked in short spurts, plus a natural immunity to small doses built up over the years. He flew high, hundreds of feet from the floor and found the control area. Through shielded glass extremely thick he made out many signs and inscriptions. All were in shapes and figures more bizarre than hieroglyphics. He was despondent. As he told me in his own words, "I have always been resourceful Josh, tenacious, capable of discovering a way through any morass, any problem. But I am completely stymied here." He was so despondent he thought I was Josh! And I wrote him back, "EA, don't give in. Look at the great things you have done for others, and the contributions. You are a saint in my mind." Even this did not cheer him. Then, Elvis popped the question: What have you learned from Master Dick? I fudged. I told him, "True I was progressing past the first stages of my training, certainly his new house was built, and a beauty it was. Master Dick had already taught me many things not just Tae. But nothing about his previous existences nor about interstellar travel. No, these were not part of the curriculum for the making of a Martial Arts Master.

Elvis began his retreat. Packed his bags and traveled first to Istanbul for his flight. But, before take-off sold the climbing gear (slightly used) back to the shop there where he bought it. Headed back to Layton.

ANOTHER FAILURE

C. Van Heyden

Thinking he'd be gone all summer Catherine was ecstatic and bubbling with joy to see him, meeting him at the airport. Elvis tried to hide his disappointment from her.

"What happened, what was your impressions of Europe?," chirped Catherine.

"I hit some very rugged country, met only very rural people, did some mountain climbing, and that's pretty much all that happened."

"But, didn't you want to tour over there?"

"I did, but factually I got sick and it sucked the fun out of my plans."

"That's a real shame. But, in celebration of your return I have prepared a little special home coming for you." Rob Dickerson, who you know and his girlfriend Sherry, plus Olivia my new best friend. So, there will be more girls than guys."

"When is it?"

"Tomorrow night!"

"Tomorrow night?...I don't think I'll be in the mood, but I'll give it my best."

"After tonight, I guarantee you'll be in the mood."

Elvis had all summer to debate with himself what he was going to do, now that he had half the total funds left that he started with. No one to commiserate with, and no one to tell of his success to either because he had none. He finally settled on, and concluded, to work all summer to fund further sorties, and to procure a radiation proof suit that could be carried lightly back to "the site", as he thought of it now. And if very lucky recover his climbing gear at the same cost as he traded it.

But Elvis hated the mundane and repetitive game of looking for a job, even if only a summer job. He'd rather be asked if he'd like to work by a professor, or businessmen in town, considering his temporal and supernal abilities together. So, he thought it.

At the party, Olivia gave him a scare. She approached Elvis and asked him if he had heard of a guy on campus counseling students in private with a strange kind of method. Elvis evaded, "Where did you hear that?"

"My boyfriend told me."

"Well, was it good for him?"

"Very good as he told it but wouldn't go into details."

"It's privileged information is why." Explained Elvis.

"That's what I thought too."

"So, Olivia, he's lucky and you're lucky too, right?"

"Why am I lucky too?"

"Because, you're his girlfriend, and if he's much better off, then you are in his closest circle."

"Oh, I get it, it rubs off as the saying goes."

"Precisely right. Have you wanted counseling?"

"Hmm...it occurred to me I might get something out of it."

"Well, I will tell you something private, and ask you to keep it that way."   "Oh, I will do that."   "I happen to know the fellow, and he taught me what he knows."   "He did, really?"   "Why don't we go into the next room? I'll tell Cathy you want to talk to me about something personal in private."   "OK."

Elvis and Olivia went into a session. When Olivia came out, she was aglow. Catherine couldn't help noticing.

"Whatever did you talk about in there?"

"Gee Catherine, we went in there for privacy, you know? But I will say that your man here is quite knowledgeable."

"Yeah, he's quite a guy, my guy." And Catherine smiled warmly.

Elvis knew he was taking a big chance, since best friends tell all, or they are not best friends. He would find out right away, one way or the other. He bet, he hoped Olivia would stay true to the covenant he made with all his applicants and not divulge any details of her session.

SUMMER JOB

C. Van Heyden

Saturday morning, Elvis got a call from Frank Bishop, Catherine's father. Frank worked for a top-flight design company in San Diego called MB Design Center. Frank asked Elvis what he was doing this summer and if he needed a job. Yes, in caps. There was an opening for an engineering student with drafting skills that opened up suddenly due to a staff member having to leave for the East coast to attend his ailing parents. Probationary of course but paid well if he lasted. Elvis faxed his transcripts immediately, and with Frank's endorsement he got the OK to start the position. He could finish his credits for graduation come the fall, giving personnel time to find a full-time replacement.

Plans suddenly leaped into view in front of Elvis. He would take the job, commute to Layton on the weekends, find a cheap motel for accommodations and save the bucks. SAVE THE BUCKS. This became a mantra, a mantra that would take him either back to the teleportation station or to CHINA or both.

Catherine was miffed, but not intensely so. Elvis and she could cuddle and spoon on the weekends, and she could have Olivia over during the week for girl things. Plus, Elvis pretended he hated to leave her which made it all the better.

With his learning rate so rapid now, although he had had only a smidgen of drafting experience, he knew he would excel.

Elvis called some 800 numbers, found a store within a hundred miles that stocked radiation protection suits. He got quotes for the range from least to most expensive. Made a record of those figures. Then he called around to several rent-a-car lots and asked what each could do for a college guy commuting to and from San Diego. Pitting one against another he finally arrived at a monthly rate lower than corporate, about $600 per month, and he could still have his pick of the brand and model. Then he places long distance called a few motels near MB Design and got quotes, telling the managers the same as the rent-a-car shops. He noticed how easy it was to get discounts, sometimes huge, by telling factually the purpose. People, the vast majority he calculated, mainly wanted to help other people if they could. Not the way his father or anyone close to him saw it when he was growing up.

Things were definitely going his way now. But as he told me.

"Damn it! I left out clothes. MB Design was a suit and tie business. That's going to set me back quite a bit at first. Two suits, shirts, new shoes, probably two pair and ties. About

$1,000 to look right and for enough shirts to go one week in the summer without laundry detail. That's my first four weeks minus food, car and rent."

If anyone could, Elvis could stretch a dollar so it looked like soft taffy. The real excitement was in the fact that he would be around full-fledged engineers, experts in metallurgy and structural physics. Who knows perhaps one of them might even have knowledge of how to build a teleportation device or be working on one.

His farewell night with Catherine, he reported, was exquisite. He also discovered during their intimate moments that Olivia had kept her promise.

C. Van Heyden

CHARLES LEXINGTON

C. Van Heyden

MB Design Center was huge, amazingly large. Three individual four story buildings linked by glass tunnels. Elvis shared an office with two other draftsmen, Chuck and Rob. They welcomed him grandly and made him feel accepted. They were in shirt sleeves. But that changed the minute they had to go out or attend any meetings in the building.

The day Elvis had dropped in on Stockton the previous summer to get the dope on him, he wore sunglasses as the floral delivery man, so now no one would recognize him.

The draftsmen worked closely with the design department, so Elvis was in contact with Frank Bishop a lot. This gave him a secure feeling in a strange environment even though he was warmly welcomed by others. Frank's speed was legendary at MB. Draftsmen could expect one to three design drawings a day from colleagues of Frank, but Frank poured in designs in batches, sometimes ten at a time. Designs from models modifying inside door panels, trunk spaces, dash accessories, outside details having to do with roof rake and grille patterns, wheel hub spacing and look. There were fourteen models for which these and other specifications changed during the design and modeling stages, not to mention for heavy machinery also produced by MB. So, there was a constant flow of documents back and forth between departments until the final designs for each model were approved by top management.

Elvis was liking his situation very much. He knew what he was really there for, and he knew that it was all right to be doing it. As predicted his first, 2nd and 3rd pay checks went to room & board, car and gas and clothes which he bought each week until he had a wardrobe. The first week he had to eat cheese sandwiches for lunch and dinner, Rice Krispies for breakfast. On that count, he relished the long eight-hour drive back to Layton each weekend, where he could revel in the cooking and glorious food that Catherine whipped up for him with love.

Elvis tried as best he could to discover any staff at MB that were "abnormal". He tried introducing in conversations in the lunchroom, when there were diners, subjects allied to space travel and Sci-Fi stories about teleportation, just to see if anyone responded. Some did, but since Madame C's list didn't contain anyone remotely near San Diego, it turned out to be a futile effort, until a visiting engineer from New York flew in.

Frank invited Elvis to lunch with the VIP and himself. What a coincidence. But Elvis didn't carry around that list so he couldn't verify if this was the same person. Nevertheless, he was going to try to steer the conversation towards his goal.

His name was Charles Lexington, very British sounding, and he was very British sounding. Seems he was responsible for the huge upswing in AM sales over the past few years, and MB snatched him with a very sweet five-year renewable contract.

When Frank left for the rest room, Elvis asked Charles what past times he enjoyed outside car engineering. Charles came back with gardening, tennis, cooking, paranormal and occult studies.

"Well, that's interesting, I have been studying in those areas too."

"You don't say. Seems everyone in the U.K. was into some kind of you know out-there subjects. It goes back to before Shakespeare, witchery and sorcery and now UFOs and such."

"I'm more interested in UFOs and, ever hear of teleportation to other planets?"

"That's a bit far-fetched for me right now." But Elvis was close enough to detect that was not even vaguely true.

"Yes, it is far-fetched, since no one has even come close to figuring out how it could be done."

"Oh, I'm sure it could be done," drolled Charles. "It's a matter of where you want to land with it. That's what makes it far-fetched to me."

"What if a person had a place they wanted to go, and not on Earth?"

"That would be interesting, indeed."

"You don't believe that an engineer of sufficient depth could bring it off, do you?"

"As I said, it's peculiarity is not in the engineering of it but it's use. Once gone from this orb, there's no saying how the "subject" could return, see?"

"What if the subject didn't need to return?"

"Then that would be it, wouldn't it, and no one would ever know, much like death."

"The Bible has it that Enoch left earth and never returned. God took him to heaven is the passage."

"Wasn't aware of that, that's in the Bible you say?"

"And the fact that 900-foot giants roamed Earth at one time also."

Frank returned.

"Really elegant rest rooms here, they even have a valet with fresh towels and a shoe-shine for 10 bucks."

"That's pretty routine in the U.K." And the conversation got back to design and specs and roll-out timetables.

Now Elvis had a comrade, at least one that could directly assist him, even if the comrade wasn't interested in traveling anywhere with it. When Elvis got back to his hotel room, he found the list and on it he found the name Mr. R.C. Lexington, New York on it. 'God truly does help those who help themselves,' loomed largely in Elvis' mind as he got horizontal for the night. Frank returned.

"Really elegant rest rooms here, they even have a valet with fresh towels and a shoe-shine for 10 bucks."

"That's pretty routine in the U.K," added Lexington. And the conversation got back to design and specs and roll-out timetables.

Now Elvis had a comrade, at least one that could directly assist him, even if the comrade wasn't interested in traveling anywhere with it. When Elvis got back to his hotel room, he found the list and on it he found the name Mr. R.C. Lexington, New York on it. 'God truly does help those who help themselves,' loomed largely in Elvis' mind as he got horizontal for the night.

C. Van Heyden

MANEUVERING

C. Van Heyden

By the second month, then late June, Elvis had stockpiled nearly a thousand dollars. He had carefully instructed payroll not to deduct anything since he was temporary, and had no job after summer, only college classes. So MB paid him as a contractor. He was tempted to buy a car for a $1000 and overall save on the monthly lease, but thousand-dollar cars were notorious for going south or needing lots of repairs constantly. Charles had flown back to N.Y. the day after their lunch, and that meant it would be still longer before Charles would or could play a role in Elvis' departure from Earth. It looked that he would continue to follow his plan, and by end of summer, if he were not replaced sooner, assemble his funds and make plans for re-visiting the Turkish mountains.

Around this time, Elvis began experiencing difficulties with drafting the complex drawings fed him by Design. They had gone easy on him the first month, knowing that he was new, but the mistakes and they were not minor were coming back to him with request for corrections at a rate he was not accustomed to. If he got himself fired, well that was it then for the summer, and that would be another delay and problem. What was startling altogether was that Stockton hadn't come into his area at all to insult and degrade, and only now and then to Frank's. Elvis didn't have the cash free to pay Chuck or Rob to handle the intricate jobs or he would have. The only solution then was to put in more time on the weekends studying the manuals and texts on drafting. He stopped visiting Layton on the weekends. Catherine freaked when she heard Elvis say he's on the ropes at MB, and more so knowing he wasn't coming home, that wasn't the effect he wanted to create.

Since his motel was only four blocks from MB Design Center, Elvis got authorization to work on the weekends, and walked over to the main building Saturday and Sunday. All he had to do was sign in at the security desk after producing his ID card and sign out each day. He got to know the main guard so well he didn't have to show his ID most of the time. Having the shop to himself without the barrage of corrections to handle immediately he was able to teach himself the finer skills relating to three-dimensional modeling. It was one skill to design or draw an exploded view of a catalytic converter and a higher skill to model that in 3D on a computer.

Having within a few weekends taught himself the necessary skills to elevate his work to the quality demanded, Elvis was secure he would reach his target, reserving the extra funds he saved by not traveling back and forth to Layton, gas, food en route and unnecessary car rental. By summer's end he had sequestered approximately four thousand dollars counting all expenses incurred, including a wardrobe, which he might even sell to a second-hand men's shop that was nearby in Layton. Either way he had accomplished the major goal he set, something which was becoming more routine in his life.

Once home in September, and a little celebratory merry-making with Catherine out of the way, Elvis set to finishing his college year in one semester, while meticulously planning his next strategies. The only thing that interrupted the scene was a call from Frank saying that MB wanted him back and was willing to pay nearly double the salary.

What had happened was what happens more and more these days, people look good on paper but don't have the ability to deliver the goods or can't solve their ownproblems within the framework of a group, and the guy hired to replace Elvis bombed after two weeks leaving before he was terminated without notifying anyone. Despite that Bingham was piloting extension type courses for graduate and undergraduates, he declined since he had wanted to stay with MB no longer than was absolutely necessary.

So he resumed classes as usual, had to decline also again invitations to call the football scores for Bingham game betters, and generally "set his cap" to look normal. He bumped into Olivia one day between classes and had quite a time maneuvering out of accepting her invitation to come over to her place for a meal, her modest exchange for his attention at the party. Finally, he got himself cloistered enough to fend off those interruptions he was so used to getting every time he embarked on a major target he wanted to accomplish. He even enlisted the secretarial skills of Catherine, filtering incoming calls and messages through her, but not outgoing.

C. Van Heyden

BANGHI PASS

C. Van Heyden

Elvis knew his best course was to return to the Bhanghi Pass and the village at its base. If he couldn't accomplish contact with the overseers of the teleport he would make his way towards Fengcheng China and be completely earnest in his inquiries with Master Chip Ty Dick. He thought that he might detour to France and hook up with Mssr. Velatrobe, but he wanted very much to visit with Joshua soon. He missed his company.

By early December Elvis had enough credits to graduate with a Bachelor of Science in space engineering. The hardest part was telling Catherine he was going on a long tour again instead of starting work. Having grown so close and so fond of her, it would be gut-wrenching to leave Earth and to leave her behind. She would be devastated.

Retracing his exact steps, he landed in Istanbul, contacted and rode in the same hired car to the village below the 10,000 foot location of the teleport. This time he wasn't carrying any of the climbing gear he brought on his first attempt.

He could not contact Bharabas for one last chance to capture some meaningful data from him. Bharabas had died. Ninety years old and no family to bury him. With the thought that his token could have been his passport to other worlds he went to talk with the town sheriff. The sheriff commiserated with Elvis but before his departure he handed him a small box, saying the old man had given it to him in case the mountain climber should return. But no matter Elvis would pierce the mystery in some way eventually by persisting if nothing else passed or no one came to help him.

Tactically the first target was to ascend the mountain and enter the hidden corridor early in the day, since previously he arrived late in the afternoon when the station was closing after a transfer occurred. He slept in the same hotel, even the same room. Early next morning he doused himself in the calendula and aloe lotion trusting that it would stick to him when his skin became the feathers of a falcon. His perception was always greater when transformed, but seeing feathers blacken would be too late a sign to escape, unlike the red prickly spots on human skin. As far as noise levels, he would take his chances knowing that the tympanum of a bird, the target organ receiving the intense vibrations, was a great deal smaller than a human one and thus less likely to be disturbed as much.

As he reported it to me: "I flew direct to the spot where the hidden entrance was concealed behind the narrow cleft in the granite peak. As I flew toward the inner cavern, I felt the building of noise and the vibrations around my wings became so great I found it difficult to maneuver. Arriving inside the main transhipping area, I perceived several large containers being hoisted through a portal that led to a much larger cube. This meant the return trip and that I had already missed the incoming freight and transportees who must have been quickly ushered down those long hallways and into a safe reception space. From there they most likely took elevators and tunnels within the mountain to exit in the village in some secret manner or in the low hills where concealment and debouche were achieved in thickets or behind outcroppings."

At this point in his report Elvis looked at me queerly. I thought he was going to say something like, "And then I spotted an overseer and was able to make contact." But he didn't. Instead he continued saying he would have tried

122

to follow the halls and tunnels to see where they lead but he was unsure he could find his way back, and they might be as contaminated with radioactive material as the main chamber. He was at an impasse again, like before and had little time to figure out what to do. If this was in fact his ultimate means of salvation, it was simultaneously his nemesis now. Short of hiring a helicopter to airlift him in a hazard suit he could not establish a safe beachhead within shot of the control room or drone living quarters. With the force field surrounding, even that method was a long shot of getting back and safely inside again.

"And so, I departed, flew back to the hotel, and changed back."

This last failure left Elvis completely down and out. He had had it well planned for success, and that he would finally come to grips with his urge to get back to Sellier and set things right. He was tired of trying.

The die was caste, and once he landed in Istanbul Elvis flew to Beijing and then road the train to Fengshan province, and from there to the hotel in Fengsheng. It left him enough to live in town for a month, long enough he expected to attain what he came for originally. He was set and sure that he would confront Master Dick, not through a via but directly and he would confess completely his intentions to him.

C. Van Heyden

RECONCILIATION

C. Van Heyden

It had been six months since Josh's last letter which told of his success in building the new home for his master. It seems that Josh also had accelerated his ability to learn and his ability to handle his duties in the year and a half since they had parted. What would it be like to get the full story from a master of Tae Kwan Do and obviously a superior being, in other regards. This occupied most of Elvis' thoughts and musings as he approached the hamlet four miles from the compound. All was as he left it, the hotel, the bookstore, the early risers at the hotel sipping white tea and enjoying succulent rice with scrambled eggs. Nobody lifting a head when he came down from his room, the same room as his first stay. The manager was as happy to see him as before and asked if he wanted to extend his stay as before. But Elvis declined saying he needn't economize this time on expenses. Once again Elvis experienced a palpable somewhat misty nostalgia for China and considered how he would probably choose, as Joshua had, to live here of all places, if he had not already resolved to right an injustice elsewhere in the cosmos.

Finally, he decided and made the four-mile trek to the new house to meet Master Dick. When he arrived, the old house was gone. Only the new home was visible and compared to the previous it was a mansion. The hedges were still there but cut down from their height of eight feet to about five. Did this mean Master Dick was through being the recluse, through with his security watch over his compound? Would he be easier to approach now because he had an able pupil proving that he was still a great teacher—that he had chosen well his acolyte and made him into the best Tae student he could be.

Master Dick warmly welcomed Elvis, as he had previously. This time it was early afternoon and Joshua was busy with his exercises in the dojang.

"It is a pleasure to see you again", Master Dick announced as he put forth his hand in the American gesture.

"Am I interrupting?" While Elvis took the master's hand and shook it firmly.

"Not in the least. How do like what you see? You know Joshua has done well by me, and I'm satisfied with the new accommodations he's constructed."

"I think it is one of the most elegantly designed houses I've yet seen. And the town is as lovely as it was when I stayed there previously. You should know that if I hadn't made other plans, I would settle in this area of China for life."

"It is a way of life not well understood and consequently not appreciated by westerners, but I perceive that you are not as the bulk of them are. Tell me about your plans, won't you?"

"Indeed, you have perceived me correctly, and that alone is comforting in a foreign land. But not very foreign now that this is my second visit."

"Joshua hinted that you had experienced some failure that was particularly distressing to you, is that why you are here again?"

"Right again Master Dick. It is that exact occurrence which has lead me back to Fengsheng and to your home. When I was here before I tried to find out the extent of your skills and powers without revealing why I wanted to know. Now, I will tell you why."

"Please come in and sit in the study while I heat a pot of white tea, you do drink it yes?"

"Of course, it is a delicacy for me, since it is practically unknown where I live."

"If it is all right with you, I can hear you well in the kitchen, can you likewise here my voice?"

"Clearly."

"Then why not go ahead and tell me why you want to have this information."

"Joshua at one time was my confessor at college. He may have told you of his reversal of goals, of his coming to realize that his most cherished desire in life was not to minister to others, but to attain a high mastery of martial arts. And it was because of my abilities, and my familiarity with my own goals that I was able to free him from his misdirected life."

"I perceived him to be completely honest in his approach, and that is why I accepted him as a pupil, even though I had retired from teaching.

"Precisely, and when Joshua informed me of your methods of instruction and some other practices, I became curious, very curious about your knowledge and powers. Enough so that I used what funds I had left to travel six thousand miles to meet you personally. You see, my goal is to leave

Earth and to acquire existence on another planet very distant from Earth named Sellier. A planet from which I was barred and expelled for crimes alleged that I did not commit. In Earth years quite a long time ago."

"Go on please."

"Since the time Joshua helped me to see my own misdeeds, my powers as a being have increased immensely, and by now you may know that I can change my shape. I can assume the shape of a falcon or other winged creature or even a quadruped if I need or desire. I can also detect, at short distances, what other beings are thinking, or trying not to think, and I can predict when absolutely necessary the future. My powers of mental concentration and observation have increased perhaps three times what they were a year and a half ago."

"I see, very impressive."

"I have used these powers to aid police to apprehend a pair of murderers, a band of bank robbers, and to free others as I have freed Josh from paths in life that they would never follow to conclusion successfully. But even with these powers, I have not yet found a way to return to Sellier, and to right the extremely unjust exile to Earth."

"You believe that I may assist you in this endeavor with my knowledge and abilities?"

"That is why I have traveled more than six thousand miles again. I traveled here via a location in Eurasia where I was able to discover the presence of extra-terrestrials and a teleport where these types of beings regularly make visits and transport cargo to and from Earth. But I was not successful in reaching these beings in a way where I could be included in the utilization of their service.   That was what distressed me."

"I see very clearly your angst and your disappointment. It is true that I have as you do the power to transform my

physical being to that of a fox or other creature as I desire. I choose fox mainly since it is emblematic of wisdom and has been through the ages."

"And I a falcon, which is and has been a symbol for freedom, a free powerful and graceful bird, a hunter. But to no avail. I sense that I am marooned here on Earth."

"We certainly all come from different parts of the universe, of this I am sure. I imagine that in a year or so I would teach or better I would as you have rekindled in Joshua the knowledge that you speak of now. And it is right that one should clean his spirit as you have done through confessions, for spiritual knowledge is of no use to one who is burdened with misdeeds, if such a person can even comprehend that knowledge and truth."

"So, you do have reality like mine?"

"I know that I have lived many lives prior to this one, in different locations and in different forms."

"Do you know where your last form was before Earth?"

"That information is not available to me."

"For myself, I was a rebel leader on Sellier, and I was accused falsely of crimes for which I was exiled to Earth."

"And some of your powers are from that period of time, I presume."

"By carefully examining my actions since and confessing the bad ones I have regained some but not all of those powers."

"And you are needing—you are looking for others who may have likewise been exiled in order to get back?"

"That has been my preoccupation for the last two years."

At that moment Master Dick fell silent and pondered.

Elvis wanted something momentous to transpire. He waited for Master Dick to speak again. It seemed to him that his entire life was held in suspension. 'No matter what comes now, I will not give up,' kept echoing in his mind.

"I believe that what you are really trying to do is right a grievous wrong, and that if you could stay here on Earth and yet somehow achieve justice back on Sellier you would be satisfied, is that so?"

"But, I don't have any reason to stay here if I can return."

"Don't you? There's at least Joshua, and he tells me that you are engaged to be married, there's that to consider."

"If I succeed in locating or developing a method of returning, I would take Catherine and Joshua with me, I would teach them what I know."

"But you presume that they would also have a strong desire to change civilizations, as you do, correct? And they may not have."

"I can live without them."

"But can you live with them? If they go only to please you or only because they feel indebted to you for the

knowledge they have attained. Then they would be marooned on Sellier, no?"

"I will find a way to go and come back, that they may have a choice which I did not have."

"But you say that you lead a revolt and a group of rebels who killed the agents of The Almighty? Were you not in effect doing things which should have gotten you exiled anyway?"

"Did Joshua tell you that?"

"I quickly gleaned what must have occurred from the generic story he told me from his life on Sellier. That story has repeated and repeated through the ages."

"What I did was wrong, but not indefensible."

"And what you have done up to now is right, and for that reason I will do what I can to help you."

"Great, then you do know how to travel to other planets?"

"I do not, but I will help you nevertheless."

C. Van Heyden

THE RACE TO PERU

C. Van Heyden

The first thing Master Dick did for Elvis was to lend him a large sum of money, knowing that he had spent his entire reserves to get to China. Master Dick, he told Elvis, could live practically without assistance from anyone, with his vegetable garden and proximity to lakes for fishing. So, with his stipend from the state he was able to put away each year approximately five hundred dollars which he occasionally used to buy a new blender or other appliance as they gave out. It was out of this fund that the supplies for his new home derived. He'd been assiduously saving for twenty-five years. His only pay back was to be informed accurately of Elvis's findings if he should succeed.

The first step Elvis took was to try to reach Serena Amparo in Peru. He did not feel confident that he could find her quickly if he first travelled there hoping to locate her home, not knowing the language nor the country. But he was certain that visiting her was much preferred over South Africa, since that area where Gingham was, was known for the sudden breakout of hostilities and much drug trafficking. He made several calls to reach her hoping that she at least spoke a bit of English and understood it well enough for him to communicate to her why he was wanting to see her. Here again Master Dick allowed him to call long distance as he needed to, to make preparations.

After several calls to the village of Santo Miraflores, he found her number. Serena spoke halting English but enough that Elvis could understand her and she barely him. Serena understood exactly what he was after. She agreed to meet with him in two weeks or sooner if he could get to Miraflores earlier. She sounded old, but he didn't ask.

Elvis informed Master Dick that he had made contact and that he was scheduling the first flight out of Beijing International. Then Master Dick really surprised him—by informing him that he would personally chauffeur him to the airport. How? In his '51 Bugatti. What on earth thought Elvis. The Master had this exotic car stashed in a flaptrap barn like building, so no one would find it or even think to look there. Gorgeous two-seater that could fly on 8-cylinders of thrust. The Master knew much faster roads than the ones Elvis used to reach Fengsheng village by rental. The journey would take a day instead of two to three. The airport had only one flight per week to Brazil. Elvis would have to go via Sydney which was longer but faster. Shanghai had delayed service to Brazil and none to Peru. On top of all he gave Elvis a code that only he knew to get a sizable discount on his airline ticket. The master had been awarded this by China Airlines years ago for instructing two of their security guards in Tae, and they had in turn taught many more airport guards those skills.

There was barely enough time to talk with Joshua, to tell him he was off before fully arriving. Josh was not shocked.

He knew how important it was and necessary Elvis' desire to settle accounts back on Sellier. He hugged and wished him much success. The entire camp would be his to guard and to utilize while Master Dick was away. This Josh had earned.

SERENA AMPARO

C. Van Heyden

Arriving late at night, after two days en route, Elvis sought shelter and the next morning for his rendezvous with Serena. When they first met, he was taken a bit by how small she was and delicate. He knew Peruvian women as were most Latin women petite, but she was almost child-like, yet clearly not a child. He had bought and brushed up on as much Castilian Spanish that he could learn in 48 hours. So, when he came into her presence, he was ready to parley.

"Buenos dias senorita Amparo. Soy, Elvis Apolliani."

"Encontada, senor. Soy Senora Amparo."

"Perdon. Senora. Permítame usar Serena?"

"Si. Esta bien."

"And now, since I speak little Spanish, as I know you know, may we converse in English?"

"Si. But I not speak good English, you know."

"Yes, but I know less Spanish than you English."

"OK."

"I am so thrilled to know what you told me on the phone."

"You mean about the flying saucers?"

"Exactly. I think I may have finally gotten to the place on Earth where I shall succeed the best. Is it true that you have spoken with them?"

"Yes, I have spoken, in so many words. And you will also, I'm sure."

"Where do we meet them?"

"They come and go almost regularly. I will show you the place."

At this moment, Elvis was electrified that he was about to meet and communicate with beings that no doubt had access to vehicles that went anywhere they wanted to go. But he couldn't go directly to them, he had to wait for them to come down and visit first. When he asked Serena what they looked like, she only said "like me". Now he knew they would not be the same beings he witnessed working at the teleportation plant. Plus, those beings probably were only able to transport him back to their planet or planets but not Sellier, since a plant would have to have been established there also.

Serena showed him a large field, fairly flat, which was their favorite landing zone. Her house was only a few hundred yards away. Serena invited Elvis to stay at her house. He accepted.

In many ways, the mien and manners of his host resembled those of Master Dick. She prepared a

Peruvian dish for him, that was a favorite in that region called Seco—a stew which is the opposite of its meaning, dry, in Spanish. They talked about the town nearby and the life she had led in it for the many years. They talked while the lamb and casaba, with rice and pinto beans, red onion, lime, cilantro and peppers simmered. Then, when they sat down to dine, she told Elvis that, "They are very curious about this planet." And further, "They, many theys, have been coming here for a very long time." Here it becamedifficult to understand her. So she called a neighbor over to translate.

This neighbor a man, quite old, but alive as any person Elvis had yet met on his journeys, translated, "It had and has been and was a stopping place before launching outward to the other galaxies since Earth is so close to the rim of this galaxy."

"My desire is to hire them to take me back to Sellier where I was expelled with no trial for crimes I did not commit."

"What will you pay them with?" translated the old man.

"I don't know right now. You say that they come and go regularly—perhaps they have not got whatthey are looking for, and I can help them find it or get it. You say they are not violent beings, right?"

"They have never hurt me or threatened me," continued the translator for Serena.

"And you say that you can easily accept their thoughts and they can yours?"

"I have never questioned it, so it remains mine to serve me or others like yourself", continued the translator.

"Then I will chance meeting them, with you of course.

The translator broke off his services at that moment and told Elvis that he would assist there also, since he had been with Serena on more than one occasion when the aliens came down.

Elvis was elated, a bit fearful still because of stories, more like rumors that because these beings were from another world, they would treat us as animals or aliens, and that meant they would not do things to benefit us as they might their own kind. Wouldn't we treat them as specimens to probe and interrogate? was what he told me was uppermost in his mind.

Elvis decided he would further accept Serena'shospitality and stay with her but only if she accepted funds in exchange. She reluctantly accepted such is the innate humanity in such a person.

The next several days Elvis tried to learn more Spanish, so that in the event that the old man was not available or, perish the thought, died between now and the appearance of aliens, he would have a better understanding of what the aliens needed to assist him. It was very hard since his head was full of conjugations not spoken Spanish, that his middle school teacher Ms. Tint enforced on him for three years in a row.

After a few weeks, while helping Serena harvest the fruit from the small orchards on her farm, he was able to grasp the simpler Spanish phrases. Her husband, he learned indirectly, had died in a local political skirmish and was buried in one of the orchards, which was her deceased husband's last request.

He became more confident of success, so much so that he wrote Josh and Master Dick that he could see the future coming and all his efforts coming to a glorious close in the remote Peruvian village.

There was one small problem left.

SAUCER BOYS

C. Van Heyden

What if the saucer beings didn't know how to get to Sellier? They must know. But where was Sellier? All that Elvis knew was that it was in the constellation Bootes and he could point the direction. But how far. Space travel required coordinates—exact coordinates. Which also included exact distances. Their attempt could be off by one tenth of one arc second and ten light years, spending an eternity searching in the wrong region of space. It's one thing to take off for a destination on a planet that's populated, where one can ask directions of natives or call home for backup but a complete impossibility to be out amongst the stars with no exact map or matrix. That's not how Elvis predicted his return as a revenant would play out. This was something even Madame C. could not deal with.

But the idea next that mushroomed up in his mind was that of R. C. Lexington, the engineer. The engineer that said to him, "It's a matter of where you want to land with it. Its peculiarity is not in the engineering of it but it's use", speaking of a teleportation device. And Elvis remembered very clearly hearing his thoughts, that as an engineer he didn't truly believe teleportation was impossible. Therefore, he wouldn't truly disbelieve in extraterrestrial visitations and transportation devices. Elvis knew that a such a visitation was imminent, he knew just as he knew who the bank robber was in San Antonio, and just as he knew which team would win the football game and by how much margin.

Elvis had not kept his number or an address. All that he knew is that MB Design had bought out his contract with AM, Aston Martin Motors? He called their head office, it was near 6:00 PM London time. Elvis got the security guard to stop the personnel director from leaving the parking lot and come back and take the call. When the director said, "Can't this wait until Monday I want to go home for the weekend?" Elvis turned up the intention.

"It is a matter of life and death that I reach Mr. Lexington tonight."

"You say you're calling from where, Peru?"

"Yes, and in less than a day or so my world will forever change for the worse if I don't reach him."

"Well, I've already missed dinner.... Let me see, no telephone number but a forwarding address in New York City for any monies and share liquidation he was owed."

Taking the prized address and after hanging up to London, Elvis dialed information in New York and asked for his number by address. None listed. 'Damn,' thought Elvis 'I've got to reach him.' He put on his sweetest manners and asked a gigantic favor of the operator.

"Can you please give me three numbers of addresses close to his?"

"I shouldn't do it but I will this one time."

Elvis called one after the other. No go. He repeated his entreaty twice more with two more operators. On the ninth call he got a person who knew R.C Lexington and his bloody number as well! Elvis had to leave a message. He left a very good one.

LEXINGTON
&
CASSANOVA

C. Van Heyden

In getting prepared for the inevitable meeting when the UFO riders made their way back to Santa Miraflores, Elvis kept at it studying Spanish, as many hours as he could take, which wasn't many since he flunked it in middle school and disliked his teacher in spades. Serena was the key and the weak link because she spoke so little English, and the idioms in Spanish always threw him, just like our sayings throw foreigners when they arrive stateside. The word "porque" means both "why?" and "because", how does that make sense? Well it does if one realizes that the answer to the question is the same question only in reverse, and by pronouncing "porque" faster it means because with the accent on the "por" and not the "que". Even if the old man wasn't sick or dead when the aliens arrive, he might not know how to say in English technical words or technical phrases that engineers and astronomers use, not to mention what saucer fly-boy alien's parley. So, Elvis kept it up and tried to talk to Serena in her language as much and as often as he could, while helping bring in the modest fruit harvest each day. He thought that she must be lonely without a husband, then dismissed that thought. She was happy with her life and she had a long life ahead of her, possibly a very long life, since who knows what she had learned from the visitors. She seemed quite young in appearance, though very petite.

A call came in from R.C. and when Elvis answered, R.C. said, "You've been looking for me?" somewhat surprised.

"I have, and I much appreciate the return call. Remember we talked over lunch for a while about things like the occult and paranormal phenomena?"

"Yep, I remember. You were telling me about teleportation, and then said something about Enoch and 900-foot giants? Yea, I do, is that what you called so urgently for?"

"Sorry, no, that's not it. But it is paranormal. I'm here living with a person who has met and communicated with aliens, and many times.

These aliens she says come down regularly and she has an ability to reach them and they her without moving the mouth."

"So, you want me to what?"

"I need your engineering background to locate a planet named Sellier and tell me the spatial coordinates."

"Do you know approximately where it is?"

"Yes, but not exactly or the exact distance, which is why I called. If I draw a map of the sky at night and place an arrow going to the destination of that planet can you get a much closer set of figures?"

"Well...I don't think I'm qualified to do it, but I do have colleagues who can."

"What would you want or they want in exchange?"

"I don't know. What are you doing with the data?"

Elvis knew it was time to spill the beans, even if it meant Lexington's derision.

"I'll lay it out flat and plain. I want these aliens to take me there."

"I see, and how will you get back?"

"I'm not coming back, it's one way."

"I see." There was a long pause. "I have a friend who is an astronomer named Casanova, and he could do the deed, I'm pretty sure. Send me a fax, and make it very clear, marked exactly and with all that you know of it."

Elvis sighed deeply but away from the mouthpiece.

"I can't ever repay you of course, because I won't be here anymore if this works."

"Well, for Mr. Casanova, perhaps a short report on the aliens would suffice.

"Yeah, that I could do. I could write it quickly and give it to Mrs. Amparo here, the contact and go-between and she could fax that when she goes into the city again."

"I'll get back to you when I have the data but be sure you are sure before you send it.

"Right...I'm sure and have been for a long time."

C. Van Heyden

GETTING READY
TO DEPART

C. Van Heyden

At the same time Elvis was joyful again, he was sweating bullets, considering how intricate this journey could be, and if he got lost why that would be it, wouldn't it. He'd wind up committing suicide probably as it was not likely he could live with the aliens on their planet and why would he want to? Holy guacamole, he didn't have any idea if he could stand space travel in a saucer, he didn't have a space suit or an oxygen breathing apparatus. God, this could turn into a debacle for sure.

Elvis started keeping a diary so that all the events leading up to and including his departure would be recorded for Mr. Casanova, for Lexington, for Catherine and Josh, and even for posterity, because even though Elvis didn't belong here he had lived here and to that degree he was tied to the inhabitants.

When he told Serena that he needed to send a fax and why she understood. That night Elvis spent most of it wrapped in a blanket studying the heavens. Waiting for the time to be the same as when the séances took place, only he knew he had to account for the huge difference in latitudes or else he would give Lexington bum data.

The next day Serena drove into town and there he made out, using a ruler and colored pens an exact picture of where he knew the planet Sellier was located, in Bootes, and he was able to use two close stars flanking where Sellier was that for sure Casanova would recognize. Then the wait.

While Elvis was waiting, he received a telegram from Josh. It read that he was impressed and gladdened that Elvis' long planned and sought return pilgrimage to Sellier was at hand. He further stated that Master Dick had found in himself a worthy successor, and because the master had no living relatives to take his position upon death, that he would be honored if Josh would accept being appointed his beneficiary. This left only Catherine. To her Elvis sent a passionate letter explaining some of the mysterious vagaries of their relationship, the trips to Europe and before, and told her he has been immeasurably happy being her steady. He sent it knowing that very likely by the time she received it he would no longer be marooned on Earth.

SELLIER

Confessions of an Alien
Marooned on Earth III

Chaz Van Heyden

The spectacular conclusion to Book I & II
Order via **Amazon at Amazon.com**
or Barnes & Noble

All letters addressed to author will be cared for immediately and answered, and can be addressed to:

Velvet Gloves Publishing
PO Box 17633
Nashville, TN 37217

Include an SASE